CONTENTS

CONTENTS

Written by Sarah E. Heller
Designed by Alfred Giuliani

3 5 7 9 10 8 6 4 2

A Catalogue record for this book is available from the British Library.

Published by Ladybird Books Ltd
80 Strand
LONDON
WC2R 0RL

http//www.ladybird.co.uk

A Penguin Company

Ladybird and the device of a Ladybird are trademarks of Ladybird Books Ltd.

Printed in Spain

Walt Disney's
The Ugly Duckling
LOST AND ALONE

*P*eck, *peck, peck,* went the tiny sound. Mother Duck felt movement beneath her. Excitedly she stood up to watch perfect fuzzy yellow heads emerge from their eggs. At last they had come into the world!

"One, two, three, four," quacked Father Duck, but one egg had not hatched yet. It was the biggest egg, the one that had made Mother Duck so uncomfortable as she perched on the nest, waiting.

Finally it started to crack open. The ducks watched expectantly. Father Duck quacked proudly until he saw a white head appear. *White!* he thought. The large duckling looked like a strange clown with a piece of egg shell on his head.

The white duckling smiled happily at his new family,
but his family did not smile back. Mother Duck was
quite upset. She hid the little yellow ducklings beneath

her wing. "Where did *this* come from?" Father Duck

quacked angrily.

Mother Duck was certain this was no child of hers.

Leading her beautiful yellow ducklings to the pond, Mother Duck kept an uncertain eye on the ugly youngster waddling along behind her.

Still, the white duckling was excited! He didn't understand that Mother Duck didn't want him around.

The poor little duckling thought the world was perfect as he climbed up onto his mother's back in the middle of the pond.

"Quack, quack, quack," said the yellow ducklings. Mother Duck smiled at them proudly.

"Honk! Honk!" said the white duckling. The others stared at him. Ducks do not make honking sounds, thought Mother Duck. She pushed the strange and

ugly white duckling off her back and swam away with her four perfect yellow ducklings.

The white duckling watched the others swimming
away from him. What did I do wrong? he wondered.
He was lonely. This great new world did not seem so
great anymore. He swam in circles all by himself.

Climbing ashore, he stopped to look at his reflection in the water. I'm an ugly duckling, he thought. My feathers are white and my neck is long. No wonder Mother Duck did not love me. The ugly duckling hung his head and wept.

He waddled through the marshes wondering what to do. "Chirp, chirp," called four friendly little birds. The ugly duckling climbed into their nest and snuggled up with them.

Then the mother bird threw a worm

to her children and the ugly duckling caught it

easily. When the mother bird saw this, she pecked and

squawked at the ugly duckling and chased him out of

the nest. The ugly duckling was so frightened that he

ran and ran. When he reached the water, he swam

without looking where he was going.

Bang! The ugly duckling hit something hard. Nervously he looked up and saw a duck. The duck was smiling. A friend, thought the duckling. He did not realise that the duck was made of wood. He happily swam around it and climbed onto its back. With a great

big bounce, he dived into the water. The wooden duck bobbed up and down, its bill hitting the duckling on the head.

Thinking his new friend was angry, the little duckling swam away. He was so sad that he didn't notice the graceful swan family swimming along nearby.

"Honk! Honk!" called the little swans curiously.

The ugly duckling looked up. These creatures look and sound just like me, he thought. They honked for him to join them and joyfully, the sad little white duckling splashed over to join his new friends.

They all played happily together. The duckling was

having so much fun that he forgot about being ugly.

He had friends now!

Soon, the mother swan drifted over. She was more

beautiful than
anything the
duckling had
ever seen.

He looked
longingly at her
graceful neck
and the white

feathered wings that curved so softly on her back. But when the little swans went to join her, he remembered that he did not belong. No one wanted an ugly duckling.

Feeling sad, he swam away. "Honk! Honk!" called his friends. They did not want him to leave. Even the mother swan came close and bent her neck, stroking him tenderly. Then something amazing happened.

She folded her wings around him in a warm embrace. "My little lost swan!" she honked joyfully.

"I'm a swan!" he said happily. "I'm not a duckling at all!" Surrounding him with their friendly faces, the swans welcomed him into his new family.

WALT DISNEY'S

Bambi

THE PRINCE IS BORN

"Wake up, Friend Owl," called Thumper, a young rabbit. "The new prince is born!" Quickly the word spread, and all of the forest animals raced to see the newborn fawn. They all cheered when he tried to stand up, but his legs were

very wobbly. "He can't walk very well," said Thumper, but the fawn's mother didn't care. She was very proud of her new son. "What're you going to call him?" asked Thumper.

"I think I'll call him Bambi," replied the doe.

Thumper nodded his approval. "That's a good name!" he said.

When it was time for Bambi to explore the forest, Thumper was happy to help his new friend.

They hopped through a hollow log and over a fallen tree. When Bambi fell down, Thumper helped him. "Stand up," he said. "You can do it!" When Bambi tried to talk, Thumper encouraged him. "That's a bird,"

Thumper pointed out. "Say *bird*." Bambi loved this big world, and he loved learning new things.

Thumper
showed him
a colourful
butterfly,
which the little
fawn followed
into a field of
pretty flowers.
Thumper

showed Bambi how to smell their beautiful fragrance.

The fawn copied his friend, but a little black nose

met his own. A friendly skunk appeared from underneath the blossoms. "Flower?" exclaimed Bambi.

Thumper exploded with laughter. "That's not a

flower," he giggled. "He's a . . ."

But the skunk interrupted. He was happy to be compared with the sweet-smelling flowers. "That's alright," he smiled, "he can call me Flower if he wants to!"

All that spring Bambi enjoyed playing with his new friends. Then one day Bambi's mother led him to the meadow. The water in the stream fascinated him. As he looked at his reflection, another face appeared beside his. It belonged to a fawn named Faline.

Bambi was startled.

He ran to where his mother stood watching and tried to hide behind her legs. But she nudged him forwards, towards Faline. "Aren't you even going to say hello?" she asked him gently.

Bambi was shy. Faline laughed gently, teasing him,

until he started to chase her. He soon discovered how much fun it was playing with Faline!

A little while later, Bambi saw some great big deer bounding through the grass. They were so fast! Bambi followed them — he liked prancing around, holding his head high as if he had antlers like the stags. Suddenly, they stopped short.

All the forest creatures became quiet. Bambi stared with the others as the great prince of the forest walked by. He was the biggest deer of them all, and his antlers were huge. Even the stags bowed their heads with

respect. But Bambi was curious. He watched in awe until the great prince turned and looked proudly at the little fawn. For Bambi was his son!

Soon spring turned to

summer, and summer to autumn. Leaves fell to the ground, and the wind blew them away. Bambi stayed warm against his mother, deep in the forest, until one morning he awoke to find the world had changed.

"Mother, why is everything white?" Bambi asked. It felt cold and wet, but Bambi didn't mind.

He was excited and ran about
trying to dodge the snow
falling from branches.
Thumper was outside playing,
too. "Bambi!" he called. "Look
what I can do!" He hopped
towards the pond and slid

onto the ice. Bambi couldn't believe his eyes!

"It's alright," Thumper assured him, thumping his
foot. "The snow's turned to ice!"

Bambi joined his friend, but his hooves slipped and

his legs sprawled out from under him. Thumper pushed and shoved to help him up, but Bambi fell again and again and again!

Next they went to find Flower. It wasn't easy to wake him up. "Why are you sleeping?" asked Bambi curiously.

"I always sleep in the winter," he yawned, before closing his eyes again.

Bambi and Thumper scampered off together into the winter wonderland. They couldn't wait to find out what wonderful new surprises life had in store.

Walt Disney's

THREE ORPHAN KITTENS

THE WORLD IS A WONDERFUL PLACE

On a farm in the country, three little kittens were born in a cosy barn where the straw was warm and comfortable. Purring contentedly, they slept with their paws wrapped around one another.

When they were old enough to move around,

the kittens discovered the farmhouse. They tiptoed playfully through the rooms. They pawed at blankets dangling from beds. They scurried after an ant that escaped between the floorboards.

Then the three little kittens climbed onto the farmer's large boot. He wasn't happy and shook his foot until they fell off.

"One cat is enough!" the farmer bellowed. He told his son to take the kittens into town. They could find homes there, he thought grouchily.

It was cold and snowy outside. The farmer's son put the kittens in a sack, threw the sack into the back of his truck and drove towards town.

The kittens thought

the bumpy ride was fun. It was cosy and dark in the sack, and they soon fell asleep. In fact, they were so content that when the farmer's son drove over a big bump and the sack flew out of the truck and into the snow, they weren't frightened at all.

The kittens emerged from the sack into a winter wonderland. It's beautiful! they thought.

Not one of them realised that they were all alone in the middle of the wintery countryside.

Scampering into the deep snow, the kittens played happily. This is so much fun! thought the white kitten, sliding down a snowdrift.

But the black and white kitten wanted to explore

and cautiously padded towards a house with an open window. The tortoiseshell kitten and the white kitten followed their brother, and they all crawled inside.

Slowly their eyes became used to the darkness and they saw

some steep stairs ahead of them. The kittens began to climb up, towards a lighted doorway.

"Miaow!" they called to each other, for the smell coming from upstairs was wonderful. As they finally stepped through the doorway, they saw a big saucer of milk.

Hungrily, they lapped it up, splattering their faces and paws.

Lick, lick, went their scratchy pink tongues, as they cleaned the milk from their fur.

Then, lifting their noses in the air, they followed a new smell coming from high above them. The three little kittens jumped up onto the table and nearly landed on top of a freshly baked pie! The crust was warm, and the juice that oozed out was sticky, but sweet and delicious as they licked it away.

The kitten's played on the table, but as they romped about, the tablecloth slid and slipped, until, CRASH! The dishes and knives and forks and spoons, and even the pie fell onto the floor. But the kittens weren't scared. The crash made a wonderful noise!

Scampering away, they found even more rooms in which to amuse themselves. Warm air coming from a grate in the floor kept the white

kitten busy while his brothers pounced and miaowed at a feather floating above.

Do, re, mi, fa, so, la, ti, went the piano as the kittens

discovered how to make music with their paws. Stepping from key to key, they were startled when a large woman appeared. They ran as she chased them, finally managing to escape into a dark cupboard.

The cupboard belonged to a little girl. It was full of toys and shoes and clothes. The kittens were exhausted from their busy day and curled up in a pair of soft pink

slippers. Soon they were fast asleep.

"What sweet little kittens!" whispered the little girl

when she found

them. Scooping all

three into a big hug,

she knew she would

love them forever.

She gave them all

names: Fluffy,

Muffy, and Tuffy.

ufasa and Sarabi were proud parents. The herds bowed as Rafiki, the wise baboon, held their cub, Simba, welcoming him to the circle of life.

"I was next in line to be king until that little *furball* was born," Mufasa's brother, Scar, spat as he watched Simba grow into a playful cub.

Simba was unaware of his uncle's feelings and even bragged to his uncle that one day he would rule the whole kingdom. Scar smiled and asked if Simba knew about the shadowy place.

"That's beyond our borders, and dangerous," Simba said.

Scar knew that the elephant graveyard, home to hyenas, would be the most perfect, and terrifying, trap for his unwanted nephew.

"Only the bravest lions go there," Scar told him.

"But I know that you are a very brave cub."

I *am* brave, he thought. I'll go there! With the help of his friend, Nala, he managed to lose their watchful guardian, Zazu, and make the journey. The cubs sang happily as they approached the elephant graveyard.

However, when hyenas began to chase them, Simba realised that not all animals honoured him as their future king. Simba tried to be brave like his father. He stood his ground and let out a roar. Suddenly Mufasa's

voice drowned out his own, and the great lion rescued the cubs.

Simba walked home in his father's footsteps, feeling very small. He had made a big mistake.

"Thank you for rescuing us, Dad. You'll always be here, won't you?" he asked.

Mufasa looked up towards the sky. "The great kings of the past look down on us from those stars," he told Simba. "They will always be there to guide you . . . and so will I."

Meanwhile, Scar was busily plotting with the hyenas. Still determined to make himself king, they

made a deal. If the hyenas would help him kill Mufasa and Simba, Scar would give them the run of the Pride Lands when he became king.

Fortunately, Scar's plan was not completely successful. Although Mufasa was killed, Simba escaped from the hyenas by running through a forest of thorns. Hurt and exhausted, the young lion cub was rescued by a warthog named Pumbaa and a meerkat called Timon.

The two friends helped Simba forget his troubles. "Hakuna matata!" they sang. "It means no worries." Soon Simba adopted their carefree attitude and put his past behind him. Learning to eat bugs, swim in the river, and play all day, the young cub slowly grew into a strong lion.

One day his old friend, Nala, came to hunt in the jungle. When Simba heard

Pumbaa call for help, he charged at Nala, but she flipped him onto his back the way she had when they used to play long ago as cubs.

"Nala?" he asked in surprise.

"Simba!" she exclaimed. "You're alive! That means you're the king!"

As they walked in the moonlight, Simba felt confused.

Seeing Nala again brought great joy but also painful memories. He felt guilty for his father's death. Nala could tell that he was troubled. The two old friends stopped to drink at

a pond and gazed at each other thoughtfully. Suddenly, Simba pulled the beautiful lioness playfully into the water and then chased her down the hill. They played again as they always had.

But Simba would not return home. Nala told him that Scar, his uncle, and the hyenas had destroyed everything. "There's no food, no water. Simba, if something isn't done soon, we will all starve."

But Simba ran away. He was frightened of going back.

Later, he heard a strange sound. Rafiki appeared. "Who are you?" Simba asked.

The wise baboon led him to a pool "The question is . . . who are *you*?" he asked. Simba looked at his reflection in the water, and saw his father, Mufasa, staring back at him. "He lives on in you!" cried Rafiki.

Mufasa's image appeared in the sky. "Remember who you are," he told Simba. "You are my son, and the one true king."

Understanding now what he must do, Simba raced

back to challenge his cruel uncle.

"Step down, Scar!" he roared. The two great lions battled while the lionesses fought off the hyenas. Using the trick that Nala had taught him, Simba flipped Scar over a cliff, and, with a great roar, reclaimed the land. From that moment on, Simba ruled the Pride Lands justly, respecting all creatures that lived in the kingdom.

In turn, the animals honoured the Lion King and his queen, Nala. One dawn, they came to pay homage to Simba's new daughter, Kiara. Simba and Nala watched proudly as Rafiki welcomed her to the circle of life.

WALT DISNEY's

THE
JUNGLE
BOOK

THE BEAR NECESSITIES

Deep in the jungle, there was a mancub crying in the tall grasses. When Bagheera, the panther, found him, he brought the boy to a wolf den.

The mother wolf willingly took in the baby, Mowgli, and raised him with her cubs. However, when Shere Khan, the tiger, returned to their part of the jungle, Mowgli was not safe anymore. The wolves decided that he must return to the man-village.

Bagheera arrived to take Mowgli back where he belonged. The boy climbed onto his back, ready for adventure — not realising where they were going. They ran all day. "Shall we turn back now?" he asked sleepily, but Bagheera shook his head.

"We're not going back this time," the panther told him.

Mowgli wanted to stay in the jungle. "I can take care of myself," he insisted.

Bagheera laughed. "You wouldn't last one day," he said as he pushed Mowgli up a tree to sleep, not realising Kaa, the

snake, was watching them. While Bagheera dozed, Kaa

looked deep into Mowgli's eyes, hypnotising him. Then, as he wrapped himself around his young victim, Bagheera opened his eyes.

"Kaa!" he roared.

The loud noise woke Mowgli.

Kaa was not happy with Bagheera. "You just made a very big mistake!" he hissed, but Mowgli managed to push his coils off the branch before he could hurt Bagheera. *Thump! Thump! Thump!* The rest of Kaa's long body followed the coils to the ground.

The next morning Bagheera was ready to continue, but Mowgli was stubborn. He held onto a tree trunk and wouldn't let go. The panther pulled him, but Mowgli kicked and struggled until Bagheera fell into the river.

"Alright. I've had it!" cried the panther. "You're on your own."

Mowgli turned and walked away. I don't need anyone, he thought moodily as he sat in the shade.

 Baloo the bear was dancing nearby but Mowgli didn't want company.

He even punched the bear when he came too close.

"Pitiful punch," said Baloo. He taught Mowgli how to fight and growl like a bear. The boy smiled at his new friend.

"You're gonna make one swell bear," said Baloo.

The mancub liked being a bear. They scratched their backs on

trees and Baloo sang as he tossed Mowgli a melon.

Mowgli even floated down the river on Baloo's tummy.

Suddenly, monkeys grabbed Mowgli! Laughing in

the trees, they tossed him back and forth. Baloo tried to

catch him, but the monkeys were fast. "Put me down!"

yelled Mowgli, but they carried him away to their king.

Baloo didn't know what to do. "HELP, Bagheera,

where are you?" the stunned bear shouted.

Deep in the jungle at the ancient ruins,

the orangutan, King
Louie, tried to make
a deal with Mowgli.
If Mowgli taught
him how to make
fire, then Mowgli
could stay in the
jungle.

"But I don't know
how to make fire,"
said the boy.

King Louie didn't believe him and danced around, trying to convince the boy to confide in him.

When Bagheera and Baloo arrived. Bagheera told Baloo to create a diversion so he could rescue the mancub. Baloo dressed up like a female monkey!

He danced with the monkeys and sidled up to King Louie, but his disguise fell off and the monkeys realised it was Baloo come to take Mowgli away! Suddenly the ancient, crumbling ruins crashed down and, in the confusion, Mowgli was rescued.

Later, as he lay sleeping, Bagheera convinced Baloo that the mancub wasn't

safe in the jungle — especially with Shere Khan, the tiger, waiting to pounce on him at any moment. Baloo knew that Bagheera was right, but he hated to see his young friend go.

The next morning Baloo and Mowgli were deep in

the jungle heading towards the man-village. Mowgli wondered where they were going. Baloo gulped. "I have to take you to the man-village. It's where you belong," he tried to explain.

Mowgli was angry. "You said we were friends!" he yelled, running away.

Lost and alone, Mowgli met Kaa.

"You must trust me if you want to stay in the jungle," hissed the snake, but Mowgli didn't trust anyone anymore.

He found a quiet place to sit and cry.

Suddenly, Shere Khan appeared! "I'm not afraid

of you," Mowgli gulped. He picked up a stick, prepared to fight, but he didn't realise how fierce Shere Khan was. The tiger lunged towards him with sharp claws and teeth!

From far away, Baloo heard the commotion and

came running. "Stop!" he cried as bravely as he could.

He grabbed Shere Khan's tail and held on tight.

Suddenly, lightning streaked across the jungle, and

soon flames were leaping high all around them.

Mowgli picked up a burning branch and tied it to Shere

Khan's tail. The mighty tiger ran for his life.

Baloo lay on the ground. Mowgli couldn't wake him up.

When Bagheera strode into the clearing he feared that

Baloo was dead and told Mowgli to try to be as brave as

Baloo had been. "Oh, Baloo!" sobbed Mowgli.

"I'm fine, Little Britches!" said Baloo suddenly.

"I was just having a rest, you know, playing it cool."

The two friends embraced happily. Then Mowgli

heard a strange voice singing. Climbing a tree for a

closer look, he saw a beautiful girl. He'd never seen another mancub before.

Baloo and Bagheera watched him follow the girl. He was happy. "Let him go," urged Bagheera, and Baloo knew it was the right thing to do.

"He would have made a great bear though!" he said.

Walt Disney's

Cinderella

IF MICE CAN BE HORSES . . .

"Wake up! Wake up!" sang the birds. But Cinderella was having a wonderful dream. She didn't want to wake up to another day of cooking, cleaning, and sewing. She pushed a little bluebird

gently with her finger, and he flew back to the window,

chirping angrily.

"Serves you right, spoiling people's dreams," Cinderella yawned. The birds and mice were her best friends. They always helped her get ready for the long day of work ahead.

Suddenly Cinderella's favourite mouse friend, Jaq, came running for help. "A visitor! A visitor!" he cried. Quickly she followed him. Indeed, there was a frightened mouse caught in a trap. "It's alright," Jaq told the mouse. "Cinderelly help you."

"You should have a name," Cinderella told the little mouse after she had rescued him.

"How about Gus?" Gus nodded happily, and Cinderella made him some tiny clothes.

After Cinderella returned to her chores, the mice and their new friend, Gus, ventured downstairs for breakfast. "Lucifee's mean!" Jaq warned, pointing to

the cat, Lucifer. Then he skilfully distracted Lucifer so

the other mice could sneak past. The mice grabbed

some corn and ran back to the safety of their hole.

Gus, however, had gathered too much corn and

couldn't carry it all. Lucifer was waiting as he scurried

to pick it all up. Suddenly he pounced.

"Miaow!" snapped Lucifer. Jaq watched in horror as the cat chased Gus and, thinking quickly, he pushed a broom onto Lucifer's head while he was distracted. Gus scurried up the tablecloth, but he wasn't out of danger. Lucifer soon had him trapped under a teacup.

Meanwhile, Cinderella hurried to get breakfast prepared. Putting teapots on trays, she carried them upstairs, unaware that Gus was trembling under one of the tea cups.

"Mother! Mother!" screamed Anastasia a few moments later. "There's a mouse under my tea cup!"

Lucky for Gus, Cinderella quickly figured out what had happened and raced to rescue Gus.

Rushing to a mouse-hole in the skirting board, Gus knew he owed his life to Cinderella.

A few days later, when an invitation came for the King's ball, Gus suggested that all of Cinderella's animal friends should help her. They knew she wanted to go to the ball, but there was no time to alter her dress.

Her stepmother kept Cinderella busy every minute.

The mice and the birds gathered needles and thread,

singing as they worked. Gus and Jaq found some

beads and ribbon that the stepsisters had discarded.

Happily, the birds stitched away. Cinderella's dress looked so beautiful!

"Thank you!" cried Cinderella when she saw it. Dressing quickly, she ran down the stairs, but her

stepsisters were jealous. "That's my sash!" said Drizella. "She's wearing my beads!" cried Anastasia, and they tore at the lovely gown until it was reduced to rags.

Poor Cinderella ran to the garden. As she sat down

and cried, her friends watched her sadly. Suddenly, the

air sparkled and
Cinderella's fairy
godmother appeared!
"Dry your tears, my
dear," she said. "You
can't go to the ball
looking like that."

With a wave of her

magic wand, an ordinary pumpkin became a shining coach. Jaq and Gus couldn't believe their eyes when suddenly they were turned into horses. "Neigh!" whinnied Gus. He was delighted to see Lucifer run away in fright.

"Now, don't forget," warned Cinderella's fairy godmother as the girl admired her sparkling new dress. "At the stroke of midnight, everything will be as it was before."

Cinderella remembered her warning, but as she danced with a handsome young man at the ball she forgot about the time. When the clock struck midnight

she ran down the steps, losing one glass slipper. "I'm sorry to be late," she apologised to her animal friends,

"but he was so wonderful."

Cinderella's friends looked at her dreamily. She had fallen in love!

The next morning there was exciting news. It was about the Prince whom Cinderella had danced with at the ball. He had fallen in love with her and was trying to find her. At that very moment the Grand Duke was trying the glass slipper on every maiden in the kingdom. Cinderella was stunned.

When her stepmother realised that Cinderella was the mystery girl, she was so jealous she locked her in the attic. "Oh, no!" cried Cinderella. "You must let me out!"

Jaq and Gus were her only chance. Bravely they stole the key and up, up, up the stairs they went, pushing and pulling the heavy key, until, breathless, they reached the top and released Cinderella.

Cinderella tried on the glass slipper and became the Prince's bride. As the happy couple ran down the steps on their wedding day, the mice and birds cheered.

DISNEY'S

101 DALMATIANS

PUPS IN DANGER

In a town house in London, there lived a handsome couple named Pongo and Perdita who loved each other very much. Their human pets, Roger and Anita,

and the cheerful housekeeper, Nanny, lived with them. They were very happy, especially Perdita. She was expecting puppies!

One stormy night the puppies arrived. Roger

puffed his pipe nervously as Pongo paced back and forth. "Fifteen puppies!" announced Nanny from the other room. She came out to congratulate Pongo. "And the mother's doing fine, love."

Pongo was overcome with pride and happiness. As Roger danced him around the room, Anita smiled happily.

"Can you believe
it, Rog? Fifteen
puppies!"

Suddenly the
door burst open!
Uninvited,
Cruella De Vil
waltzed into
the house.
"Fifteen puppies!"
she exclaimed

with an evil gleam in her eye. "How marvellous!"

Roger didn't like Cruella. When she said she wanted to buy the puppies, Roger got red in the face. "We're not selling them!" he shouted. "Not even one!"

Cruella glared at him. "Alright, keep the little beasts! But I warn you . . . you'll be sorry!"

Anita was proud of Roger for standing up to Cruella. Pongo was happy, too. He nuzzled Perdy gently as they lay with their puppies. "That dreadful

woman's gone," he told her. "The puppies are safe."

For a while, all was well. The puppies were playful and mischievous. Pongo and Perdy loved them very much.

Then one night after the puppies had gone to bed, a couple of thugs named Horace and Jasper sneaked into the house. Cruella would pay them well for this job, they thought, as they stole the sleeping

puppies and took them to an old house in the country.

When Pongo and Perdita realised the puppies had gone, they were heartbroken. They listened desperately as Roger and Anita did everything they could to find them. "Isn't there any hope?" Perdita asked Pongo.

Pongo and Perdita decided to try another way. They

used the Twilight Bark to spread the news across the city and out into the country. Had anybody seen their puppies? Finally, a reply came! Puppies had been spotted at the old De Vil place.

"Oh, Pongo, it *was* her!" cried Perdita. "Cruella stole our puppies!" They ran through the cold night, finally finding the broken-down mansion where Sergeant Tibs, a cat, was trying to keep the puppies from Horace and Jasper. It was a tough job. Cruella had found lots of other puppies too, and now there were ninety-nine!

Pongo and Perdita crashed through the window. Sergeant Tibs led the puppies away to safety while the two brave dogs fought with Horace and Jasper.

"Cruella wanted to make fur coats out of us!" cried

the puppies when Pongo and Perdita came to find them, breathless.

They had to escape immediately. "We'll go to London," said Pongo. He took a deep breath. "*All* of us!"

They began their long journey home through snow and ice. The puppies grew tired and hungry, but luckily a collie dog offered them shelter and milk in a cowshed.

Then a Labrador helped them into town.

"I've got a lift home for you all," said the Labrador,

as the Dalmatians hurried into an old blacksmith's shop. Outside was a truck that would be leaving for London shortly. But Cruella had followed them! Furious, she yelled

at Horace and Jasper, "Find them, you idiots!"

The dogs ducked low under the window as she peered inside. How would they ever get to the truck?

The puppies were playing happily until Patch pushed Lucky into the fireplace and he ended up covered in black soot! But it gave Pongo an idea.

"Let's all roll in the soot," Pongo told the puppies.

"Then we'll look like Labradors!"

At first the plan went well. In his disguise, Pongo led the puppies to the truck. Cruella watched closely from her car as he loaded them into the back but she wasn't looking for *black* puppies.

"Hurry, Perdy," called Pongo.

As she emerged

with the last of the puppies, it began to rain. *Drip, drop,* splashed the raindrops, and the soot was washed away.

"My puppies!" cried Cruella as the truck drove off.

Driving like a maniac, hair streaming behind her, Cruella followed. Horace and Jasper were racing towards the truck too, from another direction! But just in time, the driver turned off.

Crash!

Cruella's car crashed into the thugs, and over the hill they all

went together.

Pongo and Perdita were relieved. At last they could go home.

Roger and Anita were overjoyed to see them.

"Oh, Pongo!" cried Roger.

"Perdy, darling!" exclaimed Anita.

Nanny danced around the room dusting soot from the pups as she counted them — "one, two . . . ninety-eight, ninety-nine . . . a hundred and one Dalmatians!" she cried happily.

Pongo and Perdy were so happy as Roger made plans to buy a big house in the country where they could all live together as one big happy family.

Bambi

THE WINTER TRAIL

Bambi was warm and cosy in his bed. When he heard a thumping sound outside, he yawned sleepily and stepped out into the cold snow.

"C'mon, Bambi!" called Thumper. "It's a perfect day for playing."

Shaking himself awake, Bambi followed his friend. It was a beautiful day! The sky was blue and the sun was shining but the forest was covered in a blanket of snow and glittering ice.

"Look at these tracks!" said Thumper excitedly. "Who do you think they belong to?"

Bambi couldn't guess, so they decided to follow the trail. The friends pranced and hopped through the snow and before long came upon their first suspect, sitting on a branch.

"Wake up, Friend Owl!" called Thumper. Friend Owl peered at the young animals crossly. He had only just fallen asleep.

"Stop that racket!" he yelled.

Bambi and Thumper giggled. Owl was always grouchy when they disturbed his sleep. Deciding the footprints must belong to someone else, they continued on.

Next, they met up with Faline. She wanted to play.

"You can help us find out who made these tracks," said Bambi.

Thumper tried to wake up Flower, the skunk, but hibernating was serious business. "See you next spring," he told them, sleepily, his eyes still closed.

As the friends walked on, they saw a bird singing cheerfully. "Look at the pretty bird!" said Faline.

"Maybe these are *his* footprints!" But the little bird chirped no, they were far too big to be *his* footprints.

A raccoon led them towards some woodpeckers, who were busy looking for food. "We didn't make those tracks," said the noisy birds. "We don't have time for walking around down there in the snow."

"If the tracks don't belong to the woodpeckers, and they don't belong to the red bird, and they don't belong to Friend Owl, who do they belong to?" Bambi asked.

The three friends followed the trail until it ended.

"A family of quails!" exclaimed Thumper.

The mother quail and her nine babies looked up from beneath the bramble bush. "Join us," Mrs Quail cooed.

Bambi, Faline, and

Thumper were tempted to stay with the friendly birds.
But suddenly the Great Prince of the forest, Bambi's
father, appeared! He reminded them that the sun was
setting. "Go home or your mothers will worry," he told
them. Then,
just as quickly
as he had
come, he
disappeared
into the tall
trees.

"Look!" cried Bambi happily as all their mothers entered the clearing. Running under his mother's legs, the little deer stretched his nose up for a kiss.

"We've been looking for you," his mother told him tenderly.

Thumper was surprised. "How did you know how to find us?" he asked.

Mrs Rabbit pointed to tracks in the snow. Laughing, the animals followed the trail all the way home.

DISNEY'S

TARZAN®

THE BEST APE EVER

Kala loved Tarzan as if he were her natural son. When he cried, she comforted him with songs and hugs. Tarzan loved his ape mother, and she was very proud of her human child. It didn't matter that he

didn't look like everyone else.

Still, as Tarzan grew into a young boy, he was upset that he wasn't as strong or as fast as his friends.

He never stood a chance when Terk, a young gorilla, wrestled with him, and she was always leaving him behind when she went to play with her friends.

"Can I come?" Tarzan asked one day.

"Well, you could, if you could keep up," Terk answered.

She didn't expect Tarzan to follow her, but he did.

He was determined, and brave, too. When Terk dared him to get an elephant hair, he leaped off a cliff and swam into a herd of elephants.

"Piranha!" yelled a young elephant. His name was Tantor and he had never seen anything like Tarzan.

Neither had the other elephants. Frightened, they stampeded as Kerchak, the great silverback gorilla, scooped up a baby gorilla, saving it from being trampled.

"You almost killed someone," he told Tarzan sharply.

Later, Kala tried to defend her son, but Kerchak wouldn't listen. "He will never learn to be one of us!" Kerchak growled. "Look at him!"

Tarzan was deeply hurt. He ran away and splashed angrily at his own reflection in the river. As he covered himself in mud to look more like the apes in his family, Kala watched and felt very sad.

"Why am I so different?" Tarzan asked her.

Kala tenderly placed Tarzan's hand on his chest, then on her own. She explained to him that inside, their heartbeats were just the same.

"I just wish Kerchak could understand that." Kala sighed.

"I'll be the best ape ever!" he declared, hugging his mother.

True to his word, Tarzan grew into a young man with

amazing speed and strength. By imitating the animals

around him, he

learned many

skills. Finally,

he gained

Kerchak's

approval when

he defeated a

vicious enemy,

Sabor the

leopard.

As Tarzan placed the dead leopard at Kerchak's feet, he

heard a strange sound and swung

through the jungle towards it.

From a treetop, he

looked down on the first humans he had ever seen. They looked just like him!

His eyes met those of a beautiful young girl. She was terrified of the odd looking man, until he smiled at her. "Tarzan," he said, pointing to himself. "Jane," she said, pointing to herself.

Meanwhile, Terk and the others couldn't resist ransacking the human's camp. They found lots of new toys!

Tarzan and Jane became friends. She explained to him how she and her father had come to the jungle, with a guide, Clayton, to study gorillas.

Over time, Jane taught Tarzan English, while Tarzan

showed Jane the

wonders of the

jungle.

"Will you lead

us to the gorillas?"

Jane asked

Tarzan one day.

Reluctantly, he

agreed. He

realised how

much it meant to her.

When Tarzan
appeared with the
humans, Kerchak
roared. The humans
were terrified and ran
off. Kerchak was furious.
"Don't you realise?" he
said. "Humans only want to hunt and kill us."

Upset and confused, Tarzan climbed a tree and
spent the night alone.

"Why didn't you tell me that there were creatures like me?" Tarzan asked Kala the next day.

She looked at him sadly. "Because it doesn't matter." She sighed. "You're *my* son."

Though Kerchak forbade him to go near it, Tarzan was drawn to the human's camp. Every day he spent more time there, with Jane, and less time with his gorilla family.

Brokenhearted, Kala finally took Tarzan to the tree house where she had found him as a baby. "I just want you to be happy, whatever you decide," she told him.

Instinctively, she

knew what his choice would be, and her eyes filled with tears as Tarzan hugged her.

"Wherever I go, you will always be my mother," he said sadly. Then, dressed in his human clothes, Tarzan

was gone.

That night as the other gorillas slept, Kala heard a disturbing sound. Just as Kerchak had feared, some of the strange humans were

closing in on them with nets and cages. She was terrified. Not even Kerchak could protect them.

Suddenly Tarzan appeared.

As Clayton (Jane and her father's guide) picked up his gun and took aim, Tarzan snatched it from his hand and smashed it on the ground. Clayton fled.

"You saved us," said Kerchak with surprise.

"You are my *family*," Tarzan replied. The jungle friends, and Jane, soon had all the hunters caged and

the frightened animals freed.

In the struggle, Kerchak had been shot and lay dying.

"Kerchak. Forgive me," Tarzan said sadly.

"No. Forgive me for not realising that you are one of us," Kerchak replied, looking at Tarzan with respect and love. "Take care of our family . . . my son."

Realising they had never been happier than when in the jungle, Jane and her father decided to stay. The gorillas welcomed them warmly into their new family.

DISNEP'S

The Fox and the Hound

FRIENDS — NO MATTER WHAT!

Tod and Copper were best friends. Splashing and swimming, neither the fox nor the hound had a care in the world.

"We'll always be friends, won't we, Copper?" asked Tod. Hugging each other, they promised to spend every day together.

However, Amos Slade had other plans for Copper. "Teach him to behave like a hunting dog," he told his old

hound, Chief.

The next day, Tod wanted to play, and went looking for Copper.

"Who's that big dog?" he asked his friend, as he walked up to Chief, who was asleep. Sniff, sniff went Chief's big nose. Even in his sleep he knew the scent of a fox.

"Grr . . . ruff!" barked Chief. Tod was scared.

He ran fast. Amos came out with his rifle. *Bang! Bang!*

Poor Tod only just escaped into the back of Mrs. Tweed's truck. "Get off my property!" Mrs. Tweed yelled at Amos. She had taken care of Tod since he was a cub and she was concerned about him. "Amos won't let you get away next time," she said, cuddling the

frightened fox. "You'll have to stay inside."

All through the winter, Tod waited for Copper.

Big Mama, the owl, told him things would be different

after the hunting season.

One night he came back to see Copper. "You have to go, Tod!"

Copper warned. "I can't be your friend anymore."

Tod couldn't believe what he was hearing! Was it possible that Copper had forgotten all the great times they had spent together? Sadly, he turned to leave, but it was too late. Chief had woken up!

His loud barks woke Amos. "Get that fox!" yelled the hunter.

Copper couldn't let them kill Tod. Leading the hunters in the wrong direction, he tracked his friend. "Go that way," he told Tod, helping him escape.

The fox was happy. He knew Copper still cared about him. But Chief did not.

The big dog caught sight of Tod. He chased him to the big bridge, but a train was coming along the track and they were trapped.

Thinking quickly, Tod lay flat against the rails and the train passed over him. But Chief was too big to

lay flat and had to jump.

It's my fault, thought Copper as he ran to help the injured dog. Chief was just trying to protect him. Copper felt guilty and angry, but most of all he blamed Tod. As Amos planned revenge, Copper joined him.

Meanwhile, Mrs. Tweed comforted her fox. She took him to a wildlife sanctuary where he'd be safe.

"You'll be happy here," she sighed.

Poor Tod! He didn't understand. He'd lost his friend and felt frightened and alone. But Big Mama, the owl, was looking out for her friend. She called

another fox named Vixey to help Tod.

Tod had never seen anyone so beautiful! And when Big Mama appeared, Tod was over-joyed. Finally, everything would be okay.

Vixey and Tod spent the day together. She taught him how to fish. "Can I see you tomorrow?" he asked, and when Vixey nodded, he felt his heart leap.

Suddenly he heard a noise. *Snap!* It was a trap set by Amos. Tod and Vixey ran. Amos and Copper were right behind them. They crossed the great river on a fallen log. Panting and exhausted, Tod looked behind him. A bear had cornered the hunters.

Copper was in danger. Tod ran like never before and was able to distract the bear. It followed Tod onto the log, but his huge weight caused the log to tip over. Down a crashing waterfall went Tod and the bear. Weak and breathless, the fox swam to the shore.

"Now we've got him!" cried Amos, as he pointed his rifle at the little fox. But Copper stood in front of Tod. "If you want to shoot Tod, you'll have to shoot me first," said the hound.

Amos understood and walked away. Copper turned back to look at Tod. We'll always be friends, they both thought together, no matter what.

Disney · PIXAR

a bug's life

EVERY ANT HAS HIS DAY

offering stone and all the grain he had collected

disappeared into the river.

"What have you done?" Princess Atta cried, but Flik

didn't have time to answer. The grasshoppers had

crashed through the walls of the anthill.

"Where's the food?" demanded Hopper, rudely.

Princess Atta could do nothing as the bully pushed the ants around and grabbed her sister, Dot.

"I want you to collect double the amount of grain before the last leaf falls!" Hopper shouted. He didn't care that the ants would not have time to collect food for themselves, let alone him, before the rainy season began.

As the grasshoppers flew away, Flik had an idea. "We could ask bigger bugs to help us fight the grasshoppers!" he suggested. Atta agreed to let him try. She didn't really expect him to succeed, but it would keep him out of trouble for a while.

Floating away down the river on a dandelion puff, Flik waved good-bye to Princess Dot.

"He'll find the bestest, roughest bugs ever!" the little

princess told her Blueberry Scout friends.

Soon Flik returned with a group of the biggest bugs the ants had ever seen. Dot was excited.

"I knew you could do it!" she cried.

However, Princess Atta was not so pleased. "We're ants. We don't fight grasshoppers," she said to Flik. She was suspicious of the warrior bugs. Could they really defeat

Hopper and his grasshopper gang?

The large bugs were confused. "Flik! We're not warriors. We're circus performers!" cried Rosie the spider. There had been a misunderstanding. The circus bugs had thought that Flik was a talent scout and now they wanted to leave!

Flik was devastated. "Don't go!" he pleaded, grabbing Slim the stick insect. If the other ants found out that he had made another mistake, his life would be ruined. "I'll come up with a plan. You won't have to fight. Just stay!" he begged.

There wasn't time to argue. A bird had swooped down and was about to eat Dot!

Francis the ladybird caught the tiny ant princess and
Flik gathered the other circus bugs to form a rescue
party. Heimlich the caterpillar distracted the bird while
Dim, a giant blue beetle, carried them all to safety in a
thorny plant.

"Hooray!"
cried all the
ants together.
Never had the
circus bugs
heard such

applause! Even Atta herself congratulated them.

"We'll stay and help you!" the praying mantis said.

Soon the whole colony was working on Flik's latest invention. They were building a bird to chase Hopper away. Flik laughed happily as it swooped down on the grasshoppers when they next attacked.

"Watch out for the bird!" yelled Hopper to his friends. He was terrified. He and his gang quickly ran for cover. But Flik's invention was not quite perfect and the bird caught fire! When Hopper realised that the ants had tricked him he was furious!

"Ants are such losers!" he shouted, but Flik was brave and stood up to the huge, mean grasshopper.

"You're wrong!" he shouted. "You wouldn't be able to survive without us and you know it . . . don't you?"

The ant colony was furious with Flik. They knew what he said was true, but Hopper was bigger and stronger than them. As he raised his foot to crush Flik,

Atta stood in his way.

"This is the new order of things!" explained the princess. "The ants pick the food. The ants keep the food. The grasshoppers leave!"

At that moment the entire colony charged! They managed to overpower the grasshopper gang and were

about to finish off Hopper when it started to rain.

"Back to

the anthill, quickly!" shouted Atta. The weight and force of a raindrop could kill an ant. In the chaos, Hopper grabbed Flik and flew away with him through the storm.

"Flik!" cried Atta. She flew to him, and they all

landed near a real bird's nest.

Thinking it was another trick, Hopper wasn't afraid. The mother bird grabbed him – her babies were hungry and grasshoppers taste delicious!

DISNEY'S POCAHONTAS

A RACCOON, A DOG, AND A BIRD

Spoiled Percy sat on a pillow as Wiggins carried him to the ship. As the pet of Sir Ratcliffe, he was lazy and smug. Bones were his for the taking. His pillows were the finest and the fluffiest. Percy had an easy life as they sailed to the New World.

Meanwhile, across the ocean, a Native American

princess was playing with her forest friends. Meeko, a raccoon, and Flit, a hummingbird,  were her constant companions. One day as she and her two friends were swimming and diving in the big river, her friend, Nakoma, came by.

"Your father's home," she told Pocahontas. "You

must come!" Breathlessly, Meeko and Pocahontas jumped into the canoe. Flit hovered protectively as the girls steered the canoe towards home.

When they arrived, Chief Powhatan was happy to see Pocahontas. He had good news.

"Kocoum has asked for your hand in marriage," he told her proudly. "He will make a good husband."

"But, father, he's so serious," Pocahontas replied unhappily. Meeko agreed — he made a grim face, but when Flit poked his tummy he lost his balance.

However awful Pocahontas felt, the silly raccoon could always manage to make her laugh!

Still, Pocahontas was troubled. She thought that the Dream-giver must want more for her than marriage to the unsmiling Kocoum. Grandmother Willow, the wise tree spirit, thought so too, as Pocahontas explained a

dream she kept having about a spinning arrow.

"The arrow is pointing you

down your path," Grandmother Willow told her. "If you listen to the spirits around you, they will guide you."

As Pocahontas wandered through the forest, Meeko and Flit followed. Soon, they reached the sea and were met with an amazing sight; a large boat with sails that

Pocahontas mistook for clouds. They watched as one of the white men aboard came ashore and began exploring the forest. They had never seen anyone like him.

Pocahontas was curious and hid behind some bushes, but Meeko was hungry. He scurried towards the strange man and poked his nose in his bag.

"Is this what you're looking for?" asked John Smith. He gave the raccoon a

biscuit. Meeko nibbled happily.

Flit, on the other hand, was worried about Pocahontas. He pecked at the newcomer, trying to make him leave.

But Pocahontas didn't want him to go away. She felt that John had a good heart, and went to say hello. As they got to know each other, she showed him how the land and water, the people and animals, were all

connected to one

another. They

followed a bear

and listened to the

wolves. They ran

among trees and

meadows and swam with the otters. John Smith was

fascinated with all that Pocahontas had to teach.

Meeko was fascinated with John's bag. He was

greedy for more biscuits but found a compass instead.

It was too hard to bite, but he took it and hoarded his

new toy in Grandmother Willow's branches.

When the raccoon followed John Smith to his camp, there was a lot of tension in the air. The new settlers thought the Native Americans were dangerous savages and shot at any they saw. They were preparing for war.

Still, Meeko's mind was on food, and it wasn't long before he spied Percy's fine dinner. Quickly he shoved

it all into his
mouth. Percy
was furious!
Barking, the
dog chased
the raccoon

through the forest.

Their chase soon came to an abrupt halt, as they
saw signs of a terrible struggle. The local Native
Americans had taken John Smith prisoner and
sentenced him to death. Meeko, Percy and Flit

followed Pocahontas as she went to visit him.

"Whatever happens, I'll always be with you," John told her. Pocahontas was heartbroken.

"What can I do?" she asked Grandmother Willow sadly.

Meeko wanted to help, and gave her the compass he had hidden.

There was the spinning arrow from Pocahontas's dream!

Now the Native American princess knew what path to follow. Running back towards John, she threw her body over his, willing to give up her life to protect his.

She begged her father to understand that hatred was not the answer.

Chief Powhatan laid down his weapon, but Ratcliffe, trying to protect John, fired his gun at the chief.

"No!" yelled John, jumping in front of the chief.

The bullet hit him instead. Luckily, he did not die.

He would have to return to London to recover.

Pocahontas was sad, but she knew she was responsible

for keeping the peace and therefore had to stay.

Percy, Meeko, and Flit watched Pocahontas and John say their goodbyes. Even *they* were friends now.

DISNEY'S
THE LITTLE MERMAID

THERE'S NO FRIEND LIKE A FISH

"Don't be such a guppy," Ariel said to Flounder.

The little flounder was afraid of the sunken ship. It was in a deep, dark part of the ocean. But Ariel was too excited to be afraid. Here was a chance to look for human treasures for her collection.

As the little mermaid found a pipe and a fork and put them into her bag, Flounder's eyes grew large with terror.

"A shark!" he yelled.

Quickly, he swam away from the razor-sharp teeth that were chopping right through the wooden boat.

"We're going to die!" cried Flounder, as Ariel pushed him through a porthole. *Crash!* The shark was gaining on them! The shark followed the pair, but he was very big and, luckily, got stuck in a hole.

"That'll teach you, you big bully!" shouted Flounder as he followed Ariel back up to the surface. Whenever she

found human treasures, Ariel went to see Scuttle the seagull to find out more about what she had found.

Scuttle picked up the fork. "This is a dinglehopper," the silly bird said. Humans used them to comb their hair. "I haven't seen one of these for years!" he exclaimed. Calling the pipe a snarfblatt, he blew into it to make

music. But all that came out was mud and seaweed.

"That reminds me!" cried Ariel. "The concert. I'd forgotten all about it!

My father's going to be furious!"

"The concert was today?" Flounder asked. He had forgotten all about it, too, and Ariel was to be the star of the show. King Triton wasn't going to be happy.

As they hurried to the golden palace, the king and his trusted advisor, Sebastian the crab, were waiting

impatiently. "Where have you been?" they cried. "The entire celebration is ruined!"

Flounder tried to

defend Ariel. "It wasn't her fault," he declared.
"A shark chased us. Then a seagull came . . ."

"A seagull!" cried King Triton. "You went up to the
surface again to see those barbarians?"

"They're not barbarians!"
Ariel insisted.

"As long as you live
under my ocean you will
obey my rules!" he ordered.

Ariel was upset. She and
Flounder swam away to

their secret grotto, but they didn't realise that King Triton had sent Sebastian to keep an eye on them.

Sebastian listened, shocked, as Ariel sang about her dream to be part of the human world. He was amazed to see her collection of human treasures. They filled the grotto from floor to ceiling.

"What's this?" he exclaimed. "I bet your father doesn't know about this place."

Ariel pleaded with Sebastian not to tell the king, until a ship sailing above distracted her. She darted off.

"Come back!" shouted Sebastian as she swam towards the surface.

The wind began to howl. A hurricane was coming! The ship couldn't stand up to the might of the storm. When it was struck by lightening and caught fire, the sailors escaped, but Sebastian and Flounder couldn't see Ariel anywhere.

She was busy pulling a drowning human to shore. He was so handsome. He was everything Ariel had ever dreamed about!

Sebastian eventually found her singing to the unconscious prince and didn't know what to do. King Triton would explode with fury if he found out. "You must come with me and we're going to forget this ever happened," he told Ariel.

Ariel swam around for the next few days singing to

herself, dreaming of Prince Eric.

"But down here's where you belong," Sebastian said. When Flounder came to show her a statue from the shipwreck, she was delighted to see Eric's face in the stone. "It looks just like him!" she cried.

Flounder understood her dream to become human. He was the best friend a mermaid could ever have.

Disney's

The Rescuers

We Make a Great Team!

The Rescue Aid Society had gathered because someone had found a message in a bottle. It read:

To Morningside Orphanage

I am in terrible trouble.

Help, Penny

"The poor little girl!" cried Miss Bianca. "We must help her!"

She volunteered for the job and chose

Bernard to go too. "We'll make a great team!" she said.

Bernard was stunned to be chosen for such an important assignment. As he walked through the rain

holding Miss Bianca's arm, he felt like the happiest mouse alive.

They found the orphanage and scrambled inside but,

suddenly, they heard a noise.

"Cat!" cried Bianca, but it was only Rufus. "Don't worry. I'm too old to catch mice," he assured them.

Rufus loved Penny. He told them that she was sad about not being adopted, and that he didn't know where she was. "There *were* some nasty people from a

pawnshop, who tried to kidnap her once," he added.

Bernard and Bianca thought they'd better check it out. At the pawnshop, the mice discovered a school-book of Penny's. She *had* been there!

Suddenly a phone rang, startling them. An ugly woman appeared and they ran for cover.

"Can't you control that little girl?" she yelled into the phone.

"I'm coming out to Devil's Bayou on the next flight!"

Bernard and Bianca hurried to the airport. Dodging huge feet, they climbed aboard their albatross, Captain Orville. Bianca snuggled against Bernard as they flew into the sunset. What a lovely trip, thought Bernard, holding her close.

When
they reached
Devil's
Bayou, they
saw a huge
explosion!

Orville tried to dodge the fireworks but spun out of
control, crashing in the marshes.

Orville's swamp friends ran to help. They were glad
to hear the mice had come to find Penny.

"You send Evinrude to get us if you need help,"

Ellie Mae told them.

Evinrude was a drag-onfly and he had the fastest boat

around. The mice quickly climbed aboard as he steered them towards the riverboat where Penny was being kept captive.

"So you tried to run away?" they heard a man's

voice scolding as they approached. "You'd better

behave or the crocodiles will get your teddy bear!"

Poor Penny! Bernard and Bianca rushed to help,

but the crocodiles spotted them and chased the mice

smiled Bianca.

"Things will be alright," whispered Penny. Rufus had taught her about faith, and the message she put in the bottle *had* worked. Perhaps these mice *could* help.

Together they hatched a plan. Bianca was excited! But they would need help from their swamp friends. As Evinrude flew away, Bernard and Bianca hid in

Penny's dress pocket.

"Penny!" hissed the evil Medusa. "It's time to find the diamond!" They all set off towards the caves.

Penny was afraid of the dark caves. "Please don't make me go in," she pleaded.

"Get in there, or you'll never see your teddy again!" yelled the evil

Medusa as she grabbed Penny's bear.

The cave was dark and spooky. They were terrified when they came across a

large skull with gaping eyes. "That's where *I'd* hide a diamond," shivered Bernard.

Sure enough, they saw the diamond glinting deep

within the skull but they couldn't get it out.

"It's stuck fast!" said Penny. "And look! The water's

coming into the cave!"

In desperation, Bianca looked around. "There's a

sword lying over there. Use that!" she suggested.

It worked! Penny managed to prise the skull open just in time. Water filled the cave as Snoops, Medusa's assistant, hoisted them up.

"My diamond!" cried Medusa. She grabbed it and ran. Snoops and Penny followed. "Give me my bear!"

she cried.

Medusa hid

the diamond

in the bear's

stuffing and

pointed her

rifle.

"Help!" cried Penny. The Rescuers put their plan

into action. With the help of their swamp friends, they

trapped the crocodiles, tripped Medusa, and set fire to

the houseboat. Grabbing her bear, with the diamond

inside, Penny ran towards Evinrude's boat, and safety.

They cheered as they made their escape and Bianca threw her arms around Bernard. "You were fabulous!" she cried, giving him a kiss. They really did make a great team!

WALT DISNEY'S

DUMBO

THE BIGGEST EARS EVER

"Isn't he adorable?" cooed the lady circus elephants when they first saw the new baby. Mrs Jumbo was beaming with pride! Lovingly, she caressed her son with her trunk.

"Ah . . . ahh . . . CHOO!" The little elephant's sneeze shook his whole body and unravelled his large

ears. The lady elephants couldn't believe their eyes!

"What dreadful ears!" they cried,

shaking their heads
disapprovingly.

"We'll have to call him
Dumbo!" They laughed.

Mrs Jumbo was furious!
She swept her baby towards her, cuddling him
protectively. He was perfect in her eyes, and she loved
him very dearly.

Dumbo loved his mother, too. Playfully, he hid
behind Mrs Jumbo's legs, squealing with delight when
she tapped him with her trunk. And when it was time

for bed and his mother wrapped him up and rocked him to sleep, Dumbo felt safe and warm.

The next day they marched in the circus parade. People laughed when Dumbo tripped on his ears and fell in the mud.

"Hey, look at the little elephant with the big ears!" shouted a boy. He  and his friends teased Dumbo. They pulled his ears so hard that Dumbo fell over when they let go.

Trumpeting with rage, Mrs Jumbo picked up a bale of hay and threw it onto the ground.

"Crazy elephant!" shouted the frightened crowd, and Mrs Jumbo was put in chains and sent to solitary confinement. Poor Dumbo was all alone.

Heartbroken, he sat in a corner and cried while the big elephants gossiped and sniggered.

"It's all Dumbo's fault," they said. "Only a mother could love those ears!" And when the little elephant walked towards them to eat some hay, they turned their backs to him.

Poor little thing, thought Timothy Q. Mouse.

Dumbo hasn't got a friend in the whole world.

Determined to do something about it, he followed

Dumbo. "I'm your friend," he told him, offering a

peanut. "I'll help to free

your mother, but first,

let's make you a star!"

Although Timothy

tried his best, Dumbo

became a clown instead.

The other clowns

painted his face and dressed him like a baby. Pretending to rescue him from a burning building, they threw water in his face. But most humiliating of all, they pushed him from a tall tower into a bucket of water. Everyone laughed at the little elephant. Dumbo felt so ashamed.

After the show, he hung his head sadly as Timothy washed away the paint. Big tears fell down his cheeks.

"Cheer up, Dumbo!" he said. "I'm going to take you to see your mother!"

The little elephant happily followed Timothy to where his mother was being kept. She cried tears of joy as she held Dumbo, soothing him with a lullaby. When they had to say good-bye, mother and son stretched their trunks, holding onto each other for as long as they could.

That night, both Timothy

and Dumbo had strange dreams. They were awakened

by a flock of crows that were wondering how an

elephant and a mouse had managed to climb a tree!

When Dumbo opened his eyes, and saw that his

dream was true, he lost his balance. *Splash!* He and

Timothy landed in the pond below.

"How did we get into that tree?" Dumbo wondered.

"Dumbo! I think you can fly!" shouted Timothy

joyfully, pointing to Dumbo's ears.

Giving Dumbo
a feather, he
encouraged him.
"Why don't you
try it? Just flap
your ears."
Suddenly Dumbo

was in the air. He was soaring!

Dumbo and Timothy were overjoyed!

They couldn't wait to show everyone at the circus.

As Dumbo stood in the burning tower that night, he

held the little feather in his trunk. But when he jumped,

the feather slipped. He was falling fast!

"You
don't need
the feather!"
cried
Timothy.

"You can fly without it!"

Seconds before hitting the ground, Dumbo spread his ears. Up, up he flew! He did loop-the-loops. He chased clowns. Dumbo even threw peanuts at the other elephants.

"You did it!" cried Timothy. Dumbo was a star!

Soon he

was making headlines. People cheered wherever he went. But best of all, Dumbo's mother was released and they were together again!

WALT DISNEY'S

Lady and the TRAMP

A MIDNIGHT STROLL

Lady liked being a pet. Every day she woke Jim Dear for work. She brought him his slippers and fetched the newspaper. During the day, she kept his

wife, Darling, company. They enjoyed their walks together in the afternoon.

"Lady is getting so grown up," said Jim Dear one day. "I think it's time she had a new collar and lead."

When he put it on her, Lady pranced happily outside. She was excited to show her best friends, Jock and Trusty.

"Aye, you're a full-grown lady now," Jock told her.

Lady held her head high. She was so proud!

A few days later, on the other side of town, a different

kind of dog, Tramp, was rescuing his friends from the dogcatcher. "Gruff!" he barked. As the dogcatcher ran after him, his friends escaped.

Tramp loved the chase! He tricked and teased the dogcatcher until, eventually, he lost him. He looked around to see where he was. "Snob Hill," Tramp muttered. "They've got a fence around every tree."

Curious, he wandered into a yard. There was Lady and her friends.

"Jim Dear and Darling have never acted this way before," Lady was saying sadly. But Jock and Trusty smiled. They knew what the problem was. "Darling's expecting a baby," Jock told her kindly.

Lady was confused. "What's a baby?" she asked.

"Oh, they're sweet and soft," said Trusty.

But Tramp interrupted them. "When a baby moves in, the dog moves out!" he warned. Tramp didn't trust humans at all. He would never want to live as a pet behind a fence. "You'll see," he told Lady. "It'll be left-over baby food for dinner and a leaky kennel at night."

Lady was worried, but luckily Tramp's predictions did not come true. When the baby

was born, Jim Dear lifted Lady up to the cradle, while Darling pulled back the covers so she could see the tiny sleeping face. Lady loved the child instantly!

Every day she watched over the baby while Jim Dear and Darling stroked her proudly. When they decided to take a short holiday, they knew the baby would be in good hands with Lady. Besides, Aunt Sarah would be there to help.

But Aunt Sarah did not let Lady near the baby. And

worse, she brought two sly and sneaky Siamese cats. They tried to eat the goldfish. They ripped the curtains. Then they smelled milk and began creeping upstairs.

The baby! thought

Lady. Panicking, she tried to stop the cats, but her barking angered Aunt Sarah. "We're going to get you a muzzle," she said, taking Lady to the pet shop.

Lady was distraught! After the salesman put the muzzle on her, Lady ran. Cars screeched past her. As she ran, tin cans got caught on her lead and made a terrible noise. Ferocious dogs

began to chase her. Lady was terrified! She had run into a dead end!

"Grr!" growled the dogs. Suddenly, Tramp appeared! He attacked the bullies and rescued Lady. "Are you okay? What happened?" he asked her.

Sadly, Lady told her tale as Tramp listened. "First, we've got to get this muzzle off," he said, leading her to the zoo. They found

a beaver with big sharp teeth building a dam and with

one bite, Lady was free.

To cheer her up,

Tramp took her to a

special Italian restaurant.

Tony, the chef, loved

Tramp. He cooked

spaghetti and even

serenaded the dogs. As

they shared a strand of spaghetti, their noses touched.

Generously, Tramp gently rolled the last meatball towards Lady.

It was a beautiful night. Lady and Tramp walked side by side through the empty streets. The sky was lit

with stars, and the moon was full. Lying on a grassy hill in the park, the two dogs fell asleep.

The next morning, Lady was worried. "I have to get home," she cried.

Tramp shook his head. "Come with me. I'll show you what a dog's life can *really* be," he told her. "Beyond those distant hills, who knows what adventures await us."

"But who'll look after the baby?" asked Lady. So Tramp took her back to her house.

Aunt Sarah was angry with Lady for running away and chained her to the kennel. Through her tears,

Lady watched as a big rat crept into the house.

Lady barked, trying to warn Aunt Sarah about the rat. But Aunt Sarah shouted at Lady for making such a noise.

From nearby, Tramp heard her bark. "What's wrong?" he asked.

"A rat! In the baby's room!" Lady barked.

Bravely, Tramp raced into the house. Lady broke

from her chain
and followed him
up to the baby's
room and
watched as
Tramp fought the
vicious creature.

But Aunt
Sarah did not see

the rat. She just heard the crying baby. She locked Lady in the basement and Tramp in a cupboard, before calling the dogcatcher to take him away.

When Jim Dear and Darling came home the next day, they let Lady out of the basement.

She barked and whined.

"She's trying to tell us something," said Jim Dear.

Lady led Jim Dear to the rat. Tramp was a hero!

Gratefully, the humans thanked him. With a new collar and lead, Tramp became one of the smart set. He had no regrets. Soon, he and Lady were smiling as four puppies and a baby played at their feet.

Walt Disney's

OLIVER
& Company

A LITTLE LOST KITTEN

On a pavement in New York City, five kittens sat in a box. Many people walked past the box and soon, all except one tiny kitten had found homes.

"Miaow, miaow," he called sadly. It began to rain and the box soon filled with water. The little kitten jumped out, cold and wet. Still, he looked with hopeful

eyes at the people rushing past. But they were too busy, and the kitten was nearly trampled on the busy pavement. Afraid and shaking, he tried to keep out of the way.

Meanwhile, Dodger was roaming the streets looking for action. He was a street-wise dog, and when he saw an opportunity, he took it. And the wet kitten was just what he was looking for.

"Relax, kid. I don't eat cats," said Dodger. "In fact, I'm looking for a partner to

help me get some of the best sausages in town."

While the kitten distracted Louie, the hot dog seller, Dodger grabbed a string of sausages and trotted away. The furious, but brave kitten raced after him, over cars, through wet cement and a building site, to an old barge in the harbour where Dodger's friends were all waiting.

"Half of those are mine!" yelled the little cat.

Dodger and the others were very impressed by the little kitten's bravery and asked him to join their gang.

"We've never had a kitten before," said their human owner, Fagin. But they made him feel welcome. He tucked himself into the warm fur of Dodger's belly and

dreamed about finding a child to love him.

The next morning,

when the friends went in search of money to help

Fagin, they spotted a limousine. This fancy car would

do the trick, Dodger thought.

The kitten climbed inside, eager to help, but got lost!

When his friends
gave up looking for
him and ran away,
he was alone.

"It's okay, Kitty,"
said a gentle voice
from the backseat. It
was a little girl
named Jenny. She reached over to untangle the kitten
and cuddled him affectionately. The little kitten
couldn't believe it! His dream was coming true.

She took him back to her house on Fifth Avenue, and carried him to the kitchen, where she made him a special meal. She named him Oliver and got him a special name tag. They played together at the piano and even went for a walk in Central Park. Then, sitting in a rowing boat and a horse-drawn carriage, Oliver purred happily.

"I love you, Oliver," Jenny whispered that night as they lay in her warm bed.

Oliver purred contentedly. He rubbed his cheek against Jenny's, and they snuggled down to sleep. It had been a wonderful day . . . the best Oliver had ever had!

However, not everyone in the house was happy with Jenny's new pet. There was a poodle named Georgette who wanted Oliver out. So when Dodger and his

friends turned up the next day to rescue their friend, she happily threw the kitten into a bag for them.

Poor Oliver! Back at the boat he looked at the gang

with sad eyes. "I
wanted to stay
with Jenny," he
told them.

"But we

rescued you," said Dodger, confused. His feelings were

hurt. "You're a part of our family."

"I was happy there," Oliver told him. He didn't want

to upset Dodger, but Jenny was everything he'd ever

dreamed about.

Just then Fagin returned. "Fifth Avenue!" he whistled excitedly when he saw

Oliver's new name tag. *Dear very rich cat owner . . .* he wrote. He had a plan to pay back some money he owed. He would write a ransome note for Oliver.

It was dark and uncomfortable in Fagin's coat as they waited to collect the ransom money.

Soon they heard Jenny's voice. "I'm looking for my kitten," she cried, "but I'm lost."

"He's *your* kitten?" Fagin asked. He paced back and forth. This little girl was innocent and sweet. He couldn't take her money. "Don't cry," he told her, and handed Oliver over.

"Oliver!" Jenny cried. The little kitten was over-joyed to be back in her arms!

Suddenly, headlights blinded them. In a flash, Sykes, the man who Fagin owed  the money to, had grabbed Jenny, and Oliver had fallen out of her arms.

"Don't worry," Dodger promised Oliver. "We'll rescue Jenny."

Even Georgette joined the rescue party for the chase through the streets of New York. Oliver jumped into Sykes's car, but vicious dogs were ready to attack.

Racing onto a bridge, Sykes chased Fagin.

The gang rescued Jenny as they raced onto a railway bridge that had been blocked off. Then Fagin swerved onto another track. Quickly, Dodger grabbed Oliver and jumped clear

of Sykes's car just before it collided with a train.

"Thank you!" Jenny said to Dodger as she hugged Oliver tightly. Dodger knew this was where the kitten belonged. The gang joined Jenny at her birthday party. As she blew out the candles, she looked at Oliver lovingly. All of their wishes had already come true.

Walt Disney's

THE ARISTOCATS

THE BEST PLACE TO BE . . .

In a grand house in Paris lived two fine ladies . . . Madame Bonfamille and Duchess. Of course, Duchess was a cat, but she was a lady nonetheless. She was even teaching her kittens, Berlioz, Toulouse, and Marie, to be aristocats. Each day they had painting and music lessons. When the kittens teased one another, Duchess reminded them, "Real ladies and

gentlemen do not fight."

They were all very happy with Madame. She loved them so much that she decided to leave her entire fortune to her pets when she died.

Edgar, Madame's butler, was not happy; he wanted the money for himself and plotted to get rid of the cherished pets. As Edgar warmed their cream, he

added sleeping pills.
Soon Duchess
and the kittens felt
their eyes growing
heavy. Climbing into
bed, they fell fast
asleep.

That night,
Toulouse had a strange dream. He saw Edgar riding a
motorcycle. They were bouncing in a basket. Dogs
were barking. Then the basket was flying. . .

But it wasn't a dream! The Aristocats woke up in

the countryside, far from home. They were very fright-

ened. As it started to rain, they huddled in their basket.

"Poor Madame," said Duchess. "She'll be so worried

when she finds us gone."

Fortunately, the next morning was brighter. Duchess crept out of the basket to look around and was happy to see a friendly face. Strutting towards her was Mr Thomas O'Malley, a charming alley cat.

Toulouse hissed like an alley cat, while Marie just sighed dreamily. She thought Mr. O'Malley was very handsome and romantic.

Laughing, O'Malley guided them all to a road and made a mark in the dirt. "This is where our magic carpet will land to take you all home," he joked. Suddenly, a van carrying milk drove around the bend.

"All aboard for Paris!" called O'Malley.

He even made breakfast magically appear. When the

kittens closed their eyes, O'Malley uncovered a container of milk. Marie, Toulouse, and Berlioz were impressed. They all thought O'Malley was the most wonderful cat in the world!

Then suddenly the van came to a sharp halt! The angry driver had seen them and chased the cats away.

"What a horrible man!" Duchess cried.

But O'Malley knew what to do. "Paris is this way," he told them, following the train tracks.

"Clickety-clack," sang the kittens, pretending to be a train. They made their way carefully across a bridge.

Then a loud sound frightened them all. A real train

was coming!

Quickly, O'Malley pulled the kittens under the

tracks. They tried to hold on as the train rumbled

overhead, but the shaking

was too much for Marie.

With a scream, she fell

into the river below.

"Marie!" yelled

Duchess. O'Malley dived

into the water and pulled

her to safety.

"Oh, thank you, Thomas!" cried Duchess gratefully. "What would we *ever* do without you?"

That night, they arrived in the city late. The kittens were tired, so O'Malley suggested that they sleep at his house. As they walked towards the abandoned town house, they were surprised to hear music echoing

through the walls. "It's Scat Cat, and his gang!" cried

O'Malley happily.

Soon the cats were all swinging to the beat. "That's

groovy!" called

Scat Cat as

Duchess danced

with O'Malley. The

kittens had never

had so much fun!

"Stay with me?"

O'Malley asked

Duchess. They were sitting on the rooftop looking at the moon. She wished they could be together forever.

"I can't," she said reluctantly. "Madame needs us. I have to go to her."

The next morning, Duchess and the kittens went home. Edgar was not happy to see them. He stuffed the cats into a trunk.

"This time I'll get rid

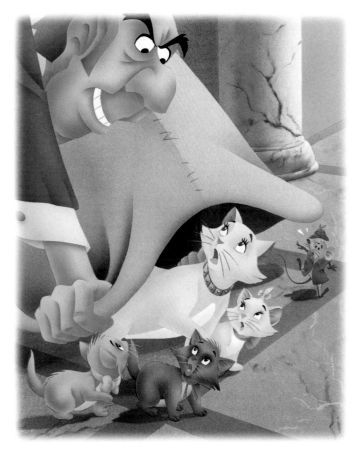

of you for good," he said, as he asked the postman to send the trunk to Timbuktu.

But O'Malley arrived just in time to save his friends.

"Hiss!" he screeched, attacking Edgar. Soon the alley cats joined the fight. Even Madame's horse gave the butler a well-deserved kick on the behind, while Roquefort, the cats' mouse friend, set Duchess and the kittens free. Then they pushed Edgar into the trunk, just as the postman arrived!

"Oh, I'm so pleased to see you all!" cried Madame as she took a photograph of the happy cats.

"Madame adopted O'Malley,

and he became part of the family. O'Malley was thrilled. He loved both Duchess and the kittens. In all his days as an alley cat, O'Malley never thought he'd settle down in a smart house like this! Yet in the whole world, there was no place he'd rather be.

THE
LION KING II
SIMBA'S · PRIDE

THE CIRCLE IS COMPLETE

Simba paced nervously back and forth. He couldn't help worrying about his daughter, Kiara. Today was her first hunt, and there were so many dangers!

When Kiara emerged from the den, Nala caressed her proudly. Even Timon and Pumbaa cried tears of joy.

"Now, Daddy," warned Kiara, "don't interfere. Promise that you'll let me do this on my own."

Simba promised reluctantly, but as Kiara left, he secretly sent Timon and Pumbaa after her. He knew The Outsiders were watching, waiting for a chance to avenge Scar, his wicked uncle. He wouldn't take any chances with his precious daughter!

On the plains, Kiara was frustrated. The animals always seemed to hear her coming. How would she ever prove that she could be independent if this hunt wasn't successful?

Determined, she chased a herd of antelope over the hill. Pumbaa and Timon tried

to keep out of sight but Kiara saw them. She was furious!

"My father sent you, didn't he!" Kiara cried. Feeling betrayed, she ran away.

But Simba had been right to worry. Zira, leader of The Outsiders, was setting a trap for Kiara. As they set

the plains on fire around her, she collapsed, exhausted, in the grass. Then a lion appeared, lifting

the lioness on his back to save her from the flames.

When Kiara opened her eyes, she was alone with the strange lion. He seemed familiar to her and she eyed him suspiciously. "Kovu?" she asked.

It *was* him! They had had so much fun as cubs . . .

until their parents had separated them. Pride Landers were not allowed to play with Outsiders. But now Kovu had saved her life. He should be allowed to return to Pride Rock.

But Simba still didn't trust Zira's son. For now,

Kovu would have to sleep outside the cave.

From a distance Zira gloated. She had taught her son to hate. As soon as he was alone with Simba, Kovu would kill his enemy.

However, Kiara unknowingly interrupted the evil plan. Excited to spend time with her childhood friend, she persuaded Kovu to give her stalking lessons.

"Did you hear me coming?" she asked, after he evaded her pounce.

"Only just," he replied. Trying to show her how it was really done, he jumped up a hill and surprised Timon and Pumbaa. The silly pair were trying to chase away a flock of birds.

"They're eating all the best bugs," moaned Pumbaa.

"Care to lend a voice?" Timon asked the lions.

With a roar, Kiara gave chase. Kovu followed easily, but he was confused. "Why are we doing this?" he asked.

Kiara laughed. "For fun!" she exclaimed.

Kovu had never done anything just for fun before. Running wildly, he roared with Kiara. It felt great until a rhino stampede chased them in the opposite direction. Ducking into a small cave, Kovu laughed with Kiara.

He had never had such a good time in all his life!

That evening, they lay in the grass looking up at the stars. Kovu felt very close to Kiara, but he was torn by his loyalty to his mother. What should he do?

Old Rafiki the baboon knew. Leading the lions to a

romantic place he called Upendi, he showed them

what was in their own hearts. Kovu and Kiara had

fallen in love!

Even Simba recognised the change in Kovu. That

night he let him sleep in the cave.

"I want to talk to you," Simba told Kovu the next day. As they went for a walk, the Lion King told Kovu the truth about Scar. Kovu couldn't believe how wrong he'd been! Determined to set things right, Kovu looked with admiration at Simba.

Then suddenly, Zira and her followers appeared.

"No!" cried Kovu, but he was knocked unconscious and the lionesses chased Simba. Desperately, he climbed a hill of loose logs and barely escaped the ambush.

The animals of the Pride Lands blamed Kovu for the

ambush. He tried to explain, but only Kiara believed

him and when he was exiled, she followed him secretly.

Kovu couldn't believe she cared so much!

Embracing her tenderly, they looked into the water.

Their

reflections

merged as

one.

"We

have to

go back,"

said Kiara

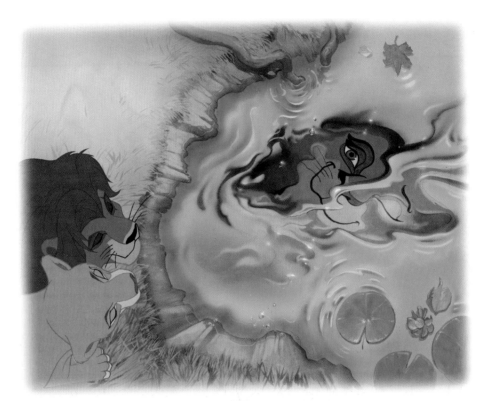

quietly. "We have to stop the fighting."

Kovu knew she was right. They returned to find the

battle about to begin.

"Stop!" cried Kiara. "Don't you see that we are one pride? We should stand together, not apart."

Simba looked at his daughter and Kovu. He could see their love. Even Zira's followers chose peace over fighting. But Zira would not give up and during a fight,

she fell into the raging river.

With her, the hate was swept away and a new peace

settled over Pride Rock. Nala and Simba warmly welcomed the new lionesses into the Pride, and they all rejoiced as Rafiki blessed the union of Kiara and Kovu.